Illustrated by Emma Chichester Clark

Piccadilly

First published in Great Britain separately
by Piccadilly Press in 1994, 1995, 1996, 1997
This edition published 2013
by Piccadilly Press,
A Templar/Bonnier publishing company
Deepdene Lodge, Deepdene Avenue,
Dorking, Surrey, RH5 4AT, UK
www.piccadillypress.co.uk

A catalogue record for this book is available
from the British Library

ISBN: 978 1 84812 329 8 (paperback)
1 3 5 7 9 10 8 6 4 2

Printed and bound by CPI Group (UK) Ltd, Croydon, CR0 4YY

Contents

MISTER MAGGS

Helen Cresswell

Chapter One

Jemima Pinchin was seven years old and lived at number twenty-eight Lime Street. She had an older brother, Jake, who was a show off, and a baby brother, Joe, who yelled a lot. Mrs Pinchin liked names beginning with the letter J. Mr Pinchin said it was lucky they weren't wanting twenty children, or she would either run out of names, or end up calling them names like Jampot or Jellybaby.

As it happened, Jemima's best friend in the whole world was called Jane. The good news was that she lived at number twenty-six Lime Street. The bad news was that her family were moving house.

When the day came, Jemima and Jane were in floods of tears. They promised they would save up all their pocket money for stamps so that they could write letters to one another every single day. They promised they would visit each other in the school holidays.

"I can't bear it!" Jemima wailed. "Oh, she's going, and she's my best friend in the world!"

"Cheer up," said Mr Pinchin. "Plenty more fish in the sea."

"Trust a girl to be a cry baby!" Jake said.

"Just look at him wave!" cried Mrs Pinchin, holding Joe high. "What a clever boy!"

"Nothing clever about waving," Jake said, and for once Jemima agreed with him.

The car turned the corner and disappeared.

"That's that, then!" said Mr Pinchin, and set off up to the shop for a paper.

That was that. This was the worst day in Jemima's whole life and nobody cared. She might as well be invisible for all the notice anyone took.

She turned and trudged back towards the house.

Crack! Whoops! She'd trodden on Joe's rattle, lying by his pram.

"Oh Jemima! *Now* look what you've done."

"It wasn't me!" Jemima blurted. "Mister Maggs did it!"

She said it before she even had time to think. She didn't know why she said it, she just did. She ran into the back garden and jumped on the swing. Everything swam into a green blur.

"That was funny!" she thought. "Mister Maggs . . . Where did *he* come from? Why's he turned up all of a sudden? Who is he, anyway?"

Then she knew.

"To be my best friend! To be my best friend in the whole world now Jane's gone!"

Chapter Two

It must be true. After all, he had turned up out of the blue to take the blame for breaking the rattle. Only a best friend would do that.

"Thanks, Mister Maggs!" she said out loud. "Like a swing?"

She climbed off and began to push the empty swing to and fro.

"You gone potty or what?"

It was Jake, getting his bike from the shed. She stuck out her tongue and carried on pushing. She soon got tired of that, though. She tried to think what games you could play with an invisible friend. She couldn't. Certainly not hide and seek. She decided to pick some flowers and arrange them in Mum's best vase, to make up for the broken rattle.

"See you later, Mister Maggs!"

She picked the best flowers she could find. Then she went to fetch the green vase. It was on the mantelpiece in the living room, and next to it was Mum's favourite ornament, a glass dolphin. Jemima had to stand on tiptoe and stretch . . . stretch . . . Whoops! Her fingers slipped and the dolphin wobbled and rocked. Jemima held her breath, and the dolphin wobbled and settled down again. It was a good job. If it had fallen and smashed on the tiled hearth, Jemima thought she might have to leave home.

In the kitchen she found Dad staring at the draining board.

"Those are my prize blooms for the show! Who's picked them?"

Jemima gulped. Her good deed had just turned into a bad deed.

"Mister Maggs! Mister Maggs did it!"

Dad went striding out into the garden to inspect his plants.

"Oh Mister Maggs," said Jemima, "you are naughty!" And she waggled her finger and giggled.

And then it happened. He came out of thin air, he shimmered out of nowhere. Jemima saw a shock of orange hair, a pointy nose and bright green eyes. He was wearing a baggy suit with red and yellow checks, with a green shirt, and red and yellow spotted bow-tie. He had twiggy fingers and black shiny shoes.

Jemima stared up at him. He was much bigger than she was. She shut her eyes. Then, slowly and fearfully, she opened them again. Still there! Starting at the shiny shoes, her eyes travelled up until they met his. He grinned and held out his hand as if to shake. Jemima slowly put out her own, then changed her mind and snatched it back.

The door opened and Mum came in. Jemima clapped her hand to her mouth and shut her eyes again, tight.

"Don't stand round under my feet, Jemima. What are all those flowers doing on the draining board?"

"Must have gone," Jemima thought, and opened her eyes. She gasped. Her mother was darting here and there about the kitchen and Mister Maggs was neatly side-stepping. As she passed him to go out again he made a sweeping bow.

"Whew!" Jemima let out a gasp of relief. "She didn't see you!"

Now he was strolling about the kitchen inspecting it. He lifted lids and peered into the cupboard. He dipped his finger into the sugar bowl and licked it. He snatched up the flowers, plonked them in the vase and filled it from the tap.

"Mister Maggs . . ." Jemima began.

He turned.

"Why . . . why exactly have you come here?"

Instead of replying he went out through the back door and into the garden.

"No! Don't! Dad's out there!"

Chapter Three

So he was, but he didn't appear to notice Mister Maggs. He seemed to look straight through him.

"Something very peculiar's going on here," thought Jemima Pinchin, who by now had quite forgotten that this was the worst day of her whole life when her best friend in the world had gone away.

In his pram Joe began to bawl. Mister Maggs went over and peered in. He pulled faces, he waggled his fingers. The crying stopped. Jemima could not work it out. Mister Maggs lifted the pram, plucked a flower from right under Mr Pinchin's nose and stuck it in his buttonhole. It clashed horribly with his suit.

"Jemima, run to the shop for me, will you?" Mum was at the back door. "Here's a bag and the money – a pack of butter, please, we need it for tea and for the picnic tomorrow."

Jemima took the bag and the money and beckoned Mister Maggs to follow her. Once they were safely out of the garden Jemima stopped.

"Why can't Mum and Dad see you?" she asked.

"And why don't you *say* something?"

A car went by. Mister Maggs waved but no one waved back.

"Can't – can't *anyone* see you except me?"

She would soon find out. PC Cobb was wheeling his bike towards them.

"Oh wow! Now what? Can you be arrested for being invisible?"

Now Mister Maggs was swinging from the wrought iron arch to the churchyard. Could he be arrested for that? She very much hoped not. She was beginning to like the jaunty Mister Maggs. And if he took the blame for everything she did wrong, she would never be in trouble again for the rest of her life.

He made her very nervous in the shop though. He strolled about, picking things up and putting

them down. He pointed at old Mrs Brown's huge flowery hat and rolled his eyes. As they went out, he tipped the *OPEN* sign on the door to *CLOSED* with a single deft twitch of a finger.

He pranced back down the street ahead of

Jemima, hands in pockets, whistling. He stopped suddenly. There, chalked on the ground, was a hopscotch game. Mister Maggs beamed. He stooped, picked up a stone and rolled it. Next minute Jemima had plonked the shopping bag on the wall and they were both playing.

Mister Maggs enjoyed himself mightily. He leaped and jumped on his grasshopper legs and waved his arms to keep his balance. The only trouble was, he was cheating.

Jemima saw him with her own eyes, though she could hardly believe it. If his pebble rolled short of the square he wanted, he merely gave a little snap of his fingers and the pebble moved, of its own accord, into the right square.

This was serious magic. Next time her pebble

rolled short, Jemima tried it herself. She didn't really expect it to work, and it didn't.

"Not playing!" she said, and marched crossly off. "You're cheating! And why don't you *say* something? Why don't you talk?"

There was no answer to that. Mister Maggs evidently didn't go in for talking.

Back home Mum was busy in the kitchen.

"You've been a long time," she said. "Where's the butter?"

Whoops! Jemima had put the bag on the wall while she played hopscotch, and there it still was – or at least, she hoped so.

"Oh, you haven't left it in the shop!"

Jemima thought fast. Before, when she had blamed Mister Maggs, she hadn't known he was there. This time, he was actually watching her. He was wagging his finger and shaking his head. But what harm could it do? He wouldn't get into trouble. No one even knew he was there. She took a deep breath.

"It wasn't my fault! It was Mister Maggs!"

He gave her a look as if to say, "Oh Jemima, what a whopper!" and Mum said, "Who *is* this Mister Maggs?" and Jake said, "She's off her rocker!" and Jemima fled to fetch the butter.

Mister Maggs seemed to be in a sulk. He marched ahead of her, and as they drew level with the hopscotch and the wall where the shopping bag was, instead of turning back he kept going. She started after him, not sure whether to be glad or sorry.

"Mister Maggs! Mister Maggs!"

He showed no sign of hearing. He just kept on going. But at least he didn't disappear. He didn't vanish into thin air. He might be back.

Chapter Four

The next day was Jake's birthday and the family was going for a picnic. His favourite present was a beautiful rainbow kite and they were going to find somewhere to fly it. Jemima made a promise to herself that if there was such a thing as being good as gold, she was going to be it – all day. If she didn't do anything to blame Mister Maggs for, perhaps he wouldn't turn up. On the other hand, she couldn't be sure.

When the family set off in the car there had been no sign of him.

"He must have gone back to where he came from," Jemima thought. "Wherever that is."

They found a perfect place to fly the kite. The car was unloaded, out came the rugs and chairs, the bat and ball and kite. Jemima helped to put out the food. First she spread the rug. Then, when no one was looking, she unscrewed a thermos and had a secret swig of orange juice. She peered into a bag and saw egg and cress sandwiches, which were her favourite. Should she pinch one?

Promises, promises, Jemima Pinchin. Who was going to be as good as gold?

She took one. It was halfway to her lips when a twiggy hand appeared out of the blue and snatched it. Jemima jumped and whirled round. She kicked the thermos and orange juice spilled all over the rug.

"Jemima!"

"Oh *now* look what you've done!"

Jemima hesitated. Mister Maggs, mouth full of egg sandwich, was frowning at her and shaking his head as if to warn her. But she took no notice.

"It wasn't me! Mister Maggs did it!"

He gave her a long, thoughtful stare. Then he wove his way between the rest of the family who were busy rescuing the food from the rug. He picked up the kite, the beautiful rainbow kite, and started to run with it. No one saw him but Jemima.

She ran after him, but by the time she reached him the kite was already up and flying. Jemima jumped and tried to pull the string from his grasp, but he laughed wickedly and the kite went higher still.

"Jemima!"

"Hey! My kite!"

Jake and Dad came running.

"Oh please, please!" Jemima gasped.

But Mister Maggs, with a gleeful smirk, tugged the string from her grasp – and let go! He watched

for a moment as the kite went sailing up into a high tree, then stuck his hands in his pockets and sauntered off.

Poor Jemima! Now it was her turn to take the blame for something she hadn't done.

"It was Mister Maggs, it was Mister Maggs!" she screamed, and for once she was telling the truth. But no one believed her. Why should they? They had seen her flying the kite with their own eyes – or thought they had.

Chapter Five

Jemima Pinchin had a terrible time after that. She had invented Mister Maggs and now she couldn't shake him off. He appeared and disappeared. Sometimes he followed her like her own shadow. And he thought of far worse things to get up to than she ever could.

For a start, he changed the time on the clock

in the kitchen. He let down both tyres on Jake's bike. He put out his foot and tripped Jemima up when she was carrying a plate of food. He put the plug in the washbasin, squirted in bubble bath and turned both taps on full.

And Jemima got all the blame. She could tell them that Mister Maggs did it till she was blue in the face, but she still had her pocket money stopped and was sent to bed early.

"Oh please, please stop it!" she begged him. "I'm sorry I blamed you, I really am!"

But never a word did he say in reply.

Then, one day, Jemima was sitting at the table doing a jigsaw puzzle and Mister Maggs was wandering about the room, fingering things, plumping cushions, switching lights on and off.

He sauntered over to the mantelpiece and tipped the glass dolphin with a finger and it began to rock.

"Oh no! Not that! Please don't!"

He looked at her very long and hard and then, with a smile, tipped the dolphin again.

Crash! Down it fell to the tiled hearth and smashed to smithereens.

Next minute Mum and Jake were there and they looked at the dolphin and then Jemima, and she looked at Mister Maggs.

He nodded. Now she knew what she must do. She took a very deep breath, then ran towards her mother.

"I did it! Oh Mum, I'm sorry – I did it!"

Mister Maggs was beaming. And then it happened. He faded. The orange hair and gaudy

suit went into a thin rainbow blur and then he had gone! Jemima didn't know whether to laugh or cry! He had, after all, been magic, and there wasn't much of that about at number twenty-eight Lime Road.

"You sure that Mister Maggs didn't do it?" Jake was saying.

"Oh no," said Jemima. "I did."

"Well, never mind," said Mum. "And thank goodness we've heard the last of that Mister Maggs. Look out of the window, Jemima, and see what's happening."

So she looked out and saw a big furniture van outside number twenty-six, and standing by it was a girl of about her own age. She turned and looked straight at Jemima and Jemima waved and the girl waved back.

"Hurray! I bet her name begins with J!" said Jemima.

Soon she had a new best friend called Julie Green and sometimes she would wonder whether she had Mister Maggs to thank. He had, after all, been a friend – sort of.

PRESS PLAY

Anne Fine

Chapter One

When the alarm went off, Nicky and Tasha sat up in their beds and stared. Mum wasn't there, but Mum's old voice recorder was on the floor by Little Joe's cot.

In front of it was a note.

Press Play, said the note.

That was all.

"Go on, then," said Tasha. "Press Play."

So Nicky slid out of bed and pressed Play. He peered through the tiny window of the recorder as the tape inside started to go round and round, and out came their mother's cheerful early morning voice.

"*Wakey-wakey!*"

"Creepy!" said Nicky, and Little Joe gripped his cot bars and pushed out his bottom lip, ready to cry, as the voice went on.

"*I had to go in to work really early today. And your dad had to work all night, so he's still sleeping.*"

"We'll have to sort ourselves out, then," muttered Tasha.

"*You'll have to sort yourselves out,*" Mum's voice echoed through the room.

Little Joe burst into tears. They spurted out so hard they missed his face completely, and fell on the carpet.

"*You'd better do Little Joe first,*" their mother's voice floated out. "*He might be a bit upset, hearing my voice, but me not being there.*"

"Too right," said Nicky, and he went across to haul Little Joe over the bars of the cot.

As soon as he felt safe in his brother's arms, Little Joe stopped crying and started to poke his fingers in Nicky's ears. Nicky dumped him down on the potty.

"I'll dress him," he said to Tasha, "if you'll feed him."

"No, no, no, no, no, no," said Tasha. "He spat porridge all down me yesterday. I'll dress him. You feed him."

"We'll toss for it," said Nicky.

He was just breaking into Tasha's money box for a coin when their mother's voice started up again.

"*Nicky, you change him. And, Tasha, you feed him.*"

"Thanks, Mum," groaned Tasha. "Thanks a bunch!"

"*Now,*" said the voice. "*While Nicky's sorting out Little Joe, Tasha can get dressed, and carry me down carefully into the kitchen.*"

"What?" Tasha said. "What is she on about?"

Nicky took Little Joe's hand and tugged him over to a pile of fresh clothes beside the cot.

"She means the recorder," said Nicky. "She means you have to carry it downstairs."

"Why?"

"I don't know," Nicky said. "So she can keep bossing us about, I suppose."

"Hmph!" said Tasha, who was always a little bit grumpy in the mornings.

Balancing the recorder carefully on top of her clean clothes, she carried the pile very carefully, as far as the top of the stairs.

Then she put the recorder down safely and went into the bathroom with her clothes.

She was just drying her face when, outside the door, she heard a strange whispering.

"What is it?" she called.

Nobody answered, but the whispering carried on.

"Is that you, Nicky?" Tasha shouted. "What do you want?"

He didn't answer, but the whispering kept up.

"Say it louder!" yelled Tasha. "I can't hear you!"

She stopped to listen. The whispering was still going on outside the door.

"Speak up!" bellowed Tasha. "Speak up! Speak up! *Speak up!*"

She flung the door open, and rushed out.

The recorder was still going. And so was her mother's voice, in a whisper.

"*. . . so remember what I say, you're not to wake Daddy up unless you really need him, so that means you've got to keep very, very quiet all the time you're in the bathroom . . .*"

"Oh, grrrr," growled Tasha.

But she growled it quietly.

Chapter Two

Little Joe sat in the highchair and banged his fist on the tray.

"Don't forget to strap him in properly," Tasha said, guessing the next bit on the recording.

"*Don't forget to strap Joe in properly,*" came the voice from the tape. "*I've made his porridge. All you have to do is heat it up.*"

Stirring the porridge, Tasha opened and closed her mouth like an actor on telly with the sound turned down while her mother's voice poured out from the recorder.

"*I hope you've chosen something sensible to wear, Tasha. It looks pretty chilly out there. I hope you're not wearing something silly like that thin cotton cowboy shirt.*"

Tasha looked down at her thin cotton cowboy shirt.

"*You should be wearing something nice and warm, like that pretty red woolly Granny knitted for you.*"

Tasha leaned over the pan full of Little Joe's porridge and pretended to throw up in it. Little Joe's eyes widened. Then he stuck out his bottom lip, ready to cry again.

"It's all right," Tasha told him. "I didn't do

anything. I was only joking. Here it comes now. Lovely porridge!"

She put the bowl on his tray, and handed him the spoon.

"Don't want it!" said Little Joe.

"Course you do," said Tasha.

"Don't!"

"Do!"

"He doesn't want it because he thinks you threw up in it," said Nicky.

Tasha turned to Little Joe. "Look," she said to him. "Watch."

Leaning over the bowl, she pretended to throw up in it all over again.

"See?" she told him. "Jokey-jokey! There's nothing wrong with the porridge."

Little Joe banged his spoon on the tray.

"Jokey-jokey!" he shouted. "Jokey-jokey!"

"He wants you to do it again," said Nicky.

"Well, he's out of luck," said Tasha.

Just at that moment, out of the recorder, their mother's voice floated across the room. "*I hope you're making sure Little Joe's eating his breakfast.*"

Sighing, Tasha did it again. Little Joe laughed so hard, his cheeks wobbled.

"Again!" he told Tasha.

"No," Tasha said. "Eat your porridge."

"Again!"

"No!"

"Again!"

Little Joe banged his spoon hard in the bowl. A great lump of porridge flew out and landed on Tasha's thin cotton cowboy shirt.

"Thank you," said Tasha. "Thank you very much."

Still dripping porridge, she slid off her seat and made for the door.

"*If you're nice to him, he shouldn't give you any trouble at all,*" the voice from the recorder assured her as she slowly climbed the stairs.

Back in the bedroom, Tasha rooted through her cupboard,

looking for something else to wear. There wasn't much. Half her clothes were in the mending pile. The other half were in the wash. In the end, just as she feared, Tasha could only find one thing.

Sighing, she pulled it over her head.

It was the pretty red woolly Granny knitted for her.

Chapter Three

Nicky stood listening to the list of things he had to get ready for Little Joe.

"*He'll need his big plastic Snoopy lunchbox,*" Mum was saying on the recorder. "*And his juice bottle. And his spare pair of underpants. And his dummy. And, of course, Rabbit.*"

Little Joe bounced up and down in his highchair. "Wabbit!" he shouted. "Wabbit! Wabbit! Wabbit!"

"Just a minute," said Nicky. "I have to find the other things as well. They're just as important as Rabbit."

"Wabbit!" Little Joe pounded his fists on the tray in front of him. "Wabbit! Wabbit! Wabbit!"

Nicky looked round. There, at the end of the table, was the big plastic Snoopy lunchbox.

"Right," he said. "That's one. Only four to go."

He kept looking. The juice bottle was nowhere to be found.

Nor were the spare pair of underpants or the dummy.

"I can't even see Rabbit," muttered Nicky.

"Wabbit!" screamed Little Joe. "Wabbit! Wabbit! Wabbit!"

"Just be quiet," Nicky told Little Joe sternly,

unstrapping him and lifting him out of the highchair. "Just yelling doesn't help. If you want to be useful, go round the house and look for things. Don't just stand there yelling Rabbit."

"Wabbit!" screeched Little Joe. "Wabbit! Wabbit! Wabbit!"

Nicky shoved his face close to Little Joe's.

"Shut up!" he yelled back. "Shut up! Shut up! Shut up!"

"Wabbit!" yelled Little Joe. "Wabbit! Wabbit! Wabbit!"

Losing his temper, Nicky snatched a tea towel off the rack and hurled it at Little Joe's head.

Furious, Little Joe snatched the big plastic Snoopy lunchbox off the table, and hurled it at Nicky.

Nicky jumped out of the way, fast.

The lunchbox landed with a crash on the floor. The clasps flew open. Out fell the juice bottle, the spare pair of underpants, the dummy and Rabbit.

"Wabbit!" shrieked Little Joe with glee. "Wabbit! Wabbit! Wabbit!"

He ran across and scooped Rabbit up in his arms. Then he sat on the floor in the corner and cuddled her, twisting one of her long velvet ears around his finger while Nicky filled the juice bottle, took the sandwich marked *Joe – Thursday* out of the fridge, and packed him a banana

and a nut bar. He was just rinsing the dummy under the tap when Tasha came down again.

"Everything going OK?" she asked him.

"Fine," Nicky said. "No problem."

Their mother's voice came from the machine. "*Right,*" it was saying. "*Quite sure you've got everything for Joe?*"

"Quite sure, thanks," Nicky told the machine grimly.

But the voice was checking them over one more time, just to be safe. "*Big plastic Snoopy lunchbox, juice bottle, spare pair of underpants, dummy and Rabbit?*"

"Wabbit!" said Little Joe ecstatically, wrapping her ear tightly around him and squeezing hard. "Wabbit! Wabbit! Wabbit!"

Chapter Four

"*Now,*" said their mother's voice. "*If you're quite sure you've have enough breakfast and you're all packed for school, it's time to reset the alarm clock for one o'clock, and put it next to Daddy's bed —*"

"Without waking him?" demanded Tasha.

"*— without waking him,*" the machine said.

"Serious stuff," said Tasha, eyeing Little Joe suspiciously.

"We'll need a plan," agreed Nicky.

First, they tried Plan A. Tasha sat Little Joe on

her knee and sang him nursery rhymes, very softly, while Nicky fetched the alarm and reset it, then crept along the landing towards the big bedroom.

Little Joe tried poking Tasha to make her sing louder. When it didn't work, he wriggled out of her lap and rushed off to fetch Nicky.

Tasha rushed after him.

Next, they tried Plan B. Tasha sneaked away with the alarm clock and Nicky sat Little Joe on the draining board and told him the story of the Three Bears while he was washing up. But Little Joe got excited when he heard the word "porridge" and banged his heels on the cupboard doors.

Nicky lifted him down, and he broke away and ran after Tasha.

In the end, they used Plan C. Tasha explained to

Little Joe that it was a game, and he had to be quiet.

"Shhh!" she said, putting a finger on her lips.

"Shhh!" said Little Joe, copying her.

"Quieter than that," warned Tasha. "Shhhhh!"

"Shhhhh!" said Little Joe, very, very quietly.

Together they went up the stairs. Nicky pushed open the door to the big bedroom.

"Shhh!" Little Joe said, but he said it quietly.

Daddy lay on his back on his side of the big bed. One arm was flung out, and his head was back. There was nasty black stubble all over his cheeks and his chin, and he was snoring loudly.

"Shhh!" Little Joe told him sternly. "Shhh!"

Nicky crept to the side of the bed and put down the alarm clock, reset for one o'clock.

Little Joe followed Nicky, and Tasha followed

Joe, in case he suddenly started fussing.

"Shhh!" Joe warned everyone.

The three of them stood in a line beside the bed and looked down at their stubbly, snoring father. Whenever he reached the main part of each breath, his whole jaw shuddered and a flap of sheet under his nose flew up in the air. There was oil on his forehead and oil under his fingernails, and his pyjamas were not buttoned up.

"Yuk," Little Joe said. "Yuk."

"Too right," said Tasha. "If this is what he looks like in the morning, good thing it's Mum who kisses us goodbye."

Just then their father snored in his sleep, smacking his lips like a chimpanzee, and letting his mouth fall wide open.

"Kiss Daddy goodbye," Nicky teased Joe.

Joe stuck out his bottom lip.

Hastily, Tasha took his hand and pulled him towards the door.

"Let's just *blow* Daddy a kiss," she said. "He'll like that. So will you."

Joe's lip went in again.

"Smart thinking, Tash," said Nicky.

The three of them stood in a line by the door, and, one by one, blew a kiss to their sleeping father. Then they left, shutting the door very quietly behind them.

Chapter Five

As soon as Little Joe had gone off to playgroup with Flora and Mrs Bundy from next door, Nicky and Tasha raced around the house, following orders from the recorder.

"*Have you turned off the taps in the bathroom properly? Especially the hot tap?*"

Nicky raced upstairs to check on the hot tap.

"*Is the cat out?*"

Tasha chased the cat out.

"*And don't forget to lock the back door.*"

Tasha locked the back door.

"*Is the oven off?*"

Nicky checked it.

"*And the grill! Don't forget the grill!*"

Nicky checked the grill – twice.

"*Is the fridge door shut?*"

"Yes," Tasha told the machine. "Yes, it's shut."

"*Have you switched your bedroom light off?*"

Now it was Tasha's turn to race upstairs.

"*And put the cat's dish out on the back-door step?*"

Nicky did that, while Tasha raced downstairs again.

"*And have you found your jackets and your school bags?*"

"Yes, yes, yes."

"*And taken your lunch money off the shelf?*"

Nicky passed one pile of coins to Tasha, and dropped the others in his pocket.

"Yes, yes, yes."

"*What else?*" the voice on the recorder said, stopping for a think.

"Have you fed the elephant?" muttered Tasha.

"And switched on the rocketship parked on the roof?" added Nicky.

"And locked Mad Old Aunty Lucy in the coal cellar?"

"With her rat poison sandwiches?"

"*I can't think of anything else,*" said the voice from the recorder. "*I hope there's nothing I've forgotten.*"

"Nicky's sub-machine gun?" suggested Tasha.

"Tasha's dirt-bike?"

"Nicky's pet armadillo?"

"Tasha's diamonds?"

"*Of course!*" the recorder said. "*Your homework reading books! They're stuck in the toast rack.*"

Nicky rushed over to fetch them.

"*That's it, then,*" said the recorder. "*I think you're probably ready to go. Now, without waking Daddy, put on your jackets, pick up your school bags and tiptoe to the front door. Drop the catch on the lock and pull the door closed behind you.*"

"Very quietly," prompted Tasha.

"*Very quietly,*" said the recorder

Together, they pulled on their jackets and picked up their school bags. They didn't wait for the voice on the recorder. They started chanting the next bit all by themselves.

"*And be good, and be careful, and stick together till you get to the main road, and make sure you cross with the lollipop lady.*"

Nicky and Tasha had finished chanting the daily speech well before the voice on the machine limped to the end.

Then they tiptoed away from the recorder towards the front door.

"*Goodbye, darlings,*" the voice called after them.

"Goodbye," called Nicky and Tasha.

They let the catch down, and pulled the door shut and locked it behind them. Then they turned to one another, and said, "Phew!"

Back in the kitchen, there was a silence as the recorded message ran on towards its end. Then, suddenly, the voice said, "*Phew!*"

And it fell silent.

A WORM'S EYE VIEW

Jan Mark

Chapter One

The allotments were behind the house, at the end of the garden, but there was no way in from there.

The council had put up a high chain-link fence. Alice and Tom could see the allotments through it. They could even see their own allotment, but it was far away, on the other side, near the hedge.

If they went upstairs to the back bedroom they

could look at their allotment properly. At the moment there were twenty green cabbages on it and fifteen red ones. Tom looked out every morning to count them, in case a cabbage thief had stolen one during the night. There were other vegetables growing on the allotment but Tom could not see them, even from the bedroom window. They were hidden behind the cabbages.

Dad worked on the allotment in the evenings, and Mum went there after lunch for an hour or two, before Alice and Tom came home from school, but on Sunday mornings they all went along together. Dad carried the spade and fork, Mum carried the rake and hoe. Tom and Alice pushed an old pram with the small tools in it. Some allotments had sheds to keep tools in, but theirs did not. Their shed was

in the garden and the garden was full of flowers. That was why they needed an allotment, to grow vegetables on.

They had to walk down Holton Road to the corner, turn right along Farmer Street, and right again at the big iron gates. There was a notice that said, *ALLOTMENTS – Private*. Tom and Alice liked that notice because although the allotments were private, they could go in. Alice always hoped that ordinary people would be walking along Farmer Street. Ordinary people could not go through the gate. That made Alice feel important.

Inside the gate were long grass lanes with allotments on both sides. Little grass paths ran between the allotments, and each allotment had a small iron notice with a number painted on it.

Alice and Tom counted as they walked along. The twenty-ninth grass path was between number fifty-four and number fifty-six. This was theirs, but they did not have to look at the numbers to know that.

Instead they looked at the backs of the houses in Holton Road and saw the one with red curtains at the upstairs windows and the pear tree in the garden. Sometimes the pear tree was white with flowers, sometimes green with leaves. Sometimes pears hung from the branches and sometimes the branches were bare – no flowers, no leaves, no pears. But they always knew where to find it. It was their pear tree, in their garden, right opposite allotment number fifty-six.

Tom and Alice wished that there was no wire fence at the end of the garden so that they could get to the allotment in two minutes instead of twenty. But they did not mind too much. They liked pushing the pram.

They thought it must be the oldest pram in the world because it was the one that Mum had ridden in when she was a baby. Sometimes they put the hood up and sat the watering can at one end, with its spout poking out. Everyone they met made the same joke.

"Taking the baby for a walk?"

Tom and Alice always made the same joke, too.

"Yes. Doesn't he look like Dad?"

This was not Dad's favourite joke.

Chapter Two

They were pushing the pram down the side entry one Sunday morning when they saw Aunty Angie at the front gate. Angie had their cousin David in a buggy. Alice thought David was too big to be in a buggy but when he was angry he would not walk and sat down in the street and went red in the face. He was usually angry.

"We're going to the allotment,"Tom said, in case Angie wanted to come in and talk to Mum. If she did that they would have to play with David who would go stiff and kick unless they let him have all the toys.

Mum and Dad came down the side entry behind them. Dad had the short, heavy tools and Mum had the long, light ones.

"Do you want us to take David along with us?" Mum said.

Tom and Alice looked at each other. Mum was fond of David. They could not think why.

"Would you mind?" Angie said. "I thought I'd take David for a walk, but I'm so tired this morning."

Angie was going to have another baby very

soon. Tom and Alice thought that David was quite enough to be going on with.

Angie went back to her house which was at the other end of the road. Tom pushed the pram on his own and Alice pushed David in the buggy. David went stiff and made angry noises. He could talk, but he preferred not to.

When they reached the iron gates and the *PRIVATE* notice, Mum let David get out of the buggy.

"You can walk on the nice grass," said Mum.

David growled and stamped on the nice grass. Every time he saw a daisy he squashed it.

At number fifty-six they parked the buggy

and the pram and Dad told them what to do.

"I am going to hoe the onions," he said. "Alice can weed round the cabbages and Tom can pull up carrots for Granny. I promised her some."

"ME," said David.

"Give him the trowel," Mum said. "He can dig a hole. I'll let him help me plant some seeds when I've finished raking."

Alice took the trowel out of the pram and gave it to David. He found some more daisies and hit them on the head.

"Dead. Dead," David said.

"Keep an eye on him," Mum said.

"Don't let him wander off."

They began to work. After a bit David started to dig.

"Plant," David said. "Now"

"In a minute," Mum said.

"NOW!"

Tom picked up a twig.

"Plant that," he said. "It might grow into a tree."

David put the twig in the hole and banged down the earth all round it.

"More plant," David said.

Alice found an old bone.

"Plant that," she said. "Perhaps you can grow a whole skeleton."

David dug another hole and planted his bone.

"More plant," David said.

Tom gave him a stone.

"That might grow into a mountain," he said. "Dig a deep hole, this time."

Alice finished weeding. She lay on the grass path and looked at the plants. "This must be what worms can see," she thought. The cabbages were so huge they hid the houses in Holton Street. The top of the onion plants looked like a high fence. The carrot tops were like giant ferns. She almost expected a dinosaur to come stomping through.

David was very quiet. He dug a whole row of holes and dropped things in. While the others were busy he went to another allotment, number sixty-five, which no one used, and dug more holes. When Tom looked round he saw David far away at number seventy-two, still digging.

Chapter Three

"Fetch him back," Dad said. "We don't want him digging up somebody's potatoes."

Alice went to get him. David did not want to come. He sat down and went stiff. Alice had to drag him all the way back to number fifty-six and his heels made two ruts in the grass.

"If we had a field," said Dad, "we could use him as a plough."

When it was time to go home, they stopped work and cleaned the tools. Alice packed the pram and Tom threw all the weeds on the compost heap. Mum put stiff, angry David in the buggy.

Dad picked up his jacket and shook it. There was no sound.

Dad's jacket always jangled with keys and loose change. He looked in the pockets.

"Have you touched my jacket?" he said.

'No," said Tom. Alice shook her head.

"I had three pounds in here," Dad said. "And where are my keys?"

"You must have dropped them," Mum said.

"They were in here when I took my jacket off," Dad said. "Someone has taken them. I don't mind about the money so much, but we need the keys."

Tom had an awful thought.

"David," he said, "did you take the keys?"

"Keys," David said. "Plant."

They all looked at him, and then they all said, "*Where?*"

"Hole," David said.

"Which hole?" Dad said.

"Big hole," David said.

"But where is the big hole?" said Mum. "Show Aunty, there's a good boy."

David went red. He held his breath. He went purple.

Chapter Four

Dad and Tom began to dig in allotment number fifty-six where David had buried the bone and the stone. Mum and Alice pushed the buggy along the bumpy grass lane to number sixty-five and number seventy-two.

"Was it here?" Alice said. "Is it there?"

David growled and clenched his fists.

Mum said, "David, we must find those keys. Try to remember where you put them."

"Big tree," David said.

Mum looked all round. "There are no big trees," she said. "There are no trees at all, except in the hedge, and those aren't big."

"He never went near the hedge," Alice said. "Perhaps he thought the keys would grow into a big tree."

She could imagine that tree, with all the keys hanging in bunches from the twigs, and clinking in the wind.

They walked back down the grass lane. Dad and Tom had found nothing.

Dad said, "David, if you do not tell me what you did with those keys, I shall be very cross."

But it was no use. Dad could not be crosser than David. No one could be crosser than David. They had to go home without the keys and Dad had to climb through the bathroom window to let them in.

Mum took David home to *his* mum, but even Angie could not make him tell where the keys were.

"Plant," David told her. "Hole. Big tree."

Alice and Tom stood in the back bedroom and stared out over the allotments, to number fifty-six. The cabbages looked very small from so far away. They could not see the carrots and onions at all.

Alice remembered how high they had seemed when she lay on the ground, like a worm. Then she thought of something. David was very small, not as small as a worm, but quite near the ground.

"Tom," she said, "even a little tree would look big to David."

"But there aren't any trees on the allotments," Tom said. "Not big or little trees."

"Perhaps it wasn't a tree at all," Alice said. "Perhaps it was just a big plant. Even tomato plants look like bushes."

They went downstairs. Mum was still at Angie's house. Dad was out in the street trying to open the car door with a bent coathanger, to get at his spare keys.

Tom and Alice ran down the garden. Tom climbed up the pear tree. Alice went to the shed and fetched the trowel and then she followed Tom. From the pear tree they stepped onto the roof of the shed and then dropped down into the allotments on the other side of the wire fence.

They were in number one hundred and forty-five. They ran along the path beside it, then past one hundred and forty-six and came to their own, number fifty-six.

"Now," said Alice, "lie down."

They lay on the grass path. On either side tall onions and carrot ferns rose up. At number fifty-three, Mr Fisk's pea sticks were a wild wood. Mrs Gray's bean rows were like a rainforest at number fifty-nine. But far away, at number seventy-four, was one strange, tall plant that looked rather like a palm tree with a knobbly trunk. It was an old cabbage that had grown too tall. Bolted, Dad said it was. No one could eat it but it was still growing.

They went over to look. The bolted cabbage

was only as tall as Alice, but to David it must have seemed like a real tree.

At the foot of the cabbage tree the earth was flat and hard, but there was one place that had been dug over. Tom took the trowel and dug again. There was a chinking sound and at the bottom of the hole they saw the keys. Alice fished them out.

"I wonder if we could find the money too," Tom said.

"I expect he put it all in different holes," Alice said. "We had better leave it and go home before Dad finds out we aren't there."

The wire fence was too high to climb so they went back down the grass lane, through the iron gate, along Farmer Street and home up Holton Road. They were just in time. Dad was still poking about with his coathanger and a policeman had stopped to see if he was stealing the car.

"That's our car and our dad," Alice said, in case the policeman was going to arrest him.

"Where have you been?" Dad said.

"Looking for David's big tree," said Tom.

"And we found it," Alice said. She held up the keys.

The policeman drove away and they all went indoors. Tom and Alice explained about the bolted cabbage and Dad rang Angie to tell Mum that the keys had been found.

"But we couldn't find the money," Alice said, when Mum came home.

"Never mind," said Mum. "We shan't starve without three pounds. It might have been three hundred pounds."

Dad said, "Wait till spring and see if it grows into a money tree. If David's right, we might all be millionaires next year."

WHY DIDN'T YOU TELL ME?

Hilary McKay

Chapter One

Nicholas Brown was eight years old. He had hair the colour of bonfire flames and freckles as big as raindrops. The gap where his two front teeth should have been had been a gap for so long that his friends could not imagine his face any other way.

He did not look the sort of boy who had mittens on strings through his coat sleeves. Or who, when party invitations arrived saying, *PLEASE WEAR OLD CLOTHES*, had no old clothes to wear. Or whose mother walked him to school every morning carrying his lunchbox (in case Nick held it the wrong way up) and kissed him goodbye right outside the school gates, in front of the lollipop lady and everyone.

But he was.

Nick had a best friend called Sam. He was such a good friend that he called for Nick every morning and walked to school with him and his mother, despite the daily risk of being kissed in front of the lollipop lady himself, which was what sometimes happened if Sam did not escape into the playground fast enough.

"You're going to have to stop her doing that," said Sam, rejoining Nick one morning after having

watched from a safe distance the dismal affair at the school gates. "That holding your hand to cross the road and the kissing anyway."

"I know," replied Nick. "I've tried. It's not easy."

It was a conversation they had often had but that day Miss Gilhoolie, their class teacher, happened to overhear as she crossed the playground.

"It's because you're a one and only, Nick!" she remarked.

"One and only what?" demanded Nick, but she had vanished into school.

"One and only what?" repeated Nick as soon as they got inside.

"Line up for assembly and stop talking!" said Miss Gilhoolie.

"One and only what?" asked Nick (who was very persistent) when assembly was over and they were all streaming back to the classroom.

"What?" asked Miss Gilhoolie. "SAMUEL OLIVER, I SAW THAT! Sorry, Nick?"

"Because I'm a one and only what?" repeated Nick patiently.

"Oh," said Miss Gilhoolie, remembering. "Child. The only one your mother has got! No wonder she doesn't want you squashed on the road!"

Nick thought this was not a reasonable thing to say. He thought of Sam and Mrs Oliver, and what she would say if Sam was squashed on the road.

"Oh never mind," he imagined Mrs Oliver saying. "I have plenty more. Three, actually. It's not as if he was a one and only!"

Somehow this did not seem very likely. And what else was Miss Gilhoolie saying?

"It was just the same for me! I was an only child like you! Carted around everywhere for years and years and years."

"How many years?" asked Nick, wondering how much longer he had still to go and thinking that eight years' carting had been plenty long enough. "How many years? More than eight?"

"Eight?" laughed Miss Gilhoolie. "More like eighteen!"

* * *

"*Another ten years?*" asked Sam at lunchtime when Nick repeated this conversation to him. "*Another ten years!*"

"That's what Miss Gilhoolie said," Nick told him gloomily.

"Another ten years," said Sam. "Another *ten* years!"

"Don't keep saying it," said Nick.

"That'll be right through Big School," remarked Sam conversationally, so Nick rugby-tackled his knees and their lunchboxes fell as they rolled together on the dining room floor.

"Another ten years!" gasped Sam, half choking on a mouthful of Nick's jumper. "That'll be right through Big Sch—"

"NICK AND SAM!" roared Miss Gilhoolie who was supervising packed-lunch dinner. "GET

UP! PICK UP THAT FOOD! IF I SEE YOU FIGHTING AGAIN . . ."

"It's all right, Miss Gilhoolie," Sam told her when Nick was no longer sitting on his chest and he could breathe again. "We weren't fighting."

"We were talking," added Nick, collecting together his packet of cheese and tomato sandwiches (labelled *Eat First*), his chocolate flapjack (labelled

Eat If You Have Finished Your Sandwiches) and wiping up his homemade yogurt with the paper napkin thoughtfully provided by his mother.

"Talking?" said Miss Gilhoolie.

"About the future," said Sam, gathering up half a pork pie, a handful of banana rusks and a jar of chocolate pudding (labelled *Suitable for babies over six months* – Sam was allowed to pack up his own lunches). "About the future, Miss Gilhoolie."

"Next lesson is games," said Miss Gilhoolie. "Any more bother from either of you and your futures will be sitting in the classroom while everyone else is outside!"

"Have a rusk," said Sam when she had gone. "They're strengthening! They give our twins strength anyway!"

"Mum never buys rusks," said Nick mournfully. "She says I'm too old. And for chocolate pudding."

"Tell her it's full of vitamins," said Sam. "Look! It says so on the label."

"She'd rather make yogurt."

"Another ten years of homemade yogurt," said Sam. "And being taken to school and kissed in front of the lollipop lady, and packed lunches with labelled sandwiches! What you need . . . Get off, Miss Gilhoolie's looking! I wasn't being horrible, I was just saying! What you need is a baby."

"A baby?"

"Then you wouldn't be a one and only!"

"A baby!" repeated Nick, and wondered why he had never thought of it before.

Chapter Two

"A baby?" said Nick's mother.

"Or two," said Nick. "Or three. Mrs Oliver has three besides Sam!"

"Mrs Oliver is a saint," said Nick's mother.

"A baby?" asked Nick's father. "Do you know what a baby would mean? Half as much of everything! Pushchairs in the hall. Crying at night. Keeping quiet while it's asleep . . . "

"It would be worth it," said Nick.

"Worth it?"

"Not to be a one and only."

"I always *wanted* to be a one and only," said Nick's father.

"You wouldn't have if you were one," said Nick.

Once Nick had got an idea into his head, he wasn't the sort of person to forget it. Or to let anyone else forget it. Sam fell ill and was off school for a week and without him Nick felt more of a one and only than ever and redoubled his campaign to acquire a baby in the house.

After a few days of Nick's efforts, his parents grew very weak and broke down to the point of saying, "Well, you never know," and "Perhaps you're right," and "Well, we'll have to see."

After a few weeks they seemed to give up completely.

"Yes, Nick," they said. "We have been thinking

about it and you are quite right. But babies do not arrive all at once and it is early days yet."

"Early days for what?"

"To talk about me having a baby."

"Are you having a baby?" asked Nick.

"Well, I hope so," said his mother cautiously. "One day."

"One day!" said Sam when Nick repeated this conversation.

"Don't you think it might be working?"

"When I ask if we can go on a safari holiday and whether I can have a television in my bedroom or anything like that, they always say 'One day'," said Sam. "And one day never comes. Perhaps they're just saying it to shut you up. If you don't mind me saying, your mum is looking jolly thin – just look at her beside mine!"

Nick looked across the playground. There was his mother, almost eclipsed by large, rosy Mrs Oliver standing beside her.

"And don't forget the airport!" said Sam.

"Oh," said Nick, deflating suddenly. "Oh yes."

The airport had been at the beginning of Nick and Sam's friendship. It had come about as the result of enormous pestering by Nick (backed up by Sam) and aimed at Nick's father. The subject had been aeroplanes, and the sad fact that Nick and Sam were the only boys in their class never to have been on one. Or even to have seen one, close up. Or even to have visited an airport.

And at the end of the pestering (which had

lasted for several hours) Nick's father had grabbed both boys, stuffed them in his car, driven them to the nearest airport, parked them in window seats overlooking the airfield with instructions not to move, disappeared, and returned with a flight schedule.

They had sat, temporarily silenced by the combined fierceness and amazing generosity of Nick's father, and waited all afternoon for their flight to be called.

And at the end of the afternoon Nick's father had said proudly, "Now you can't say you've never seen an aeroplane close up!" and had driven them home, never suspecting that he had not given them a stunningly brilliant afternoon.

Which was why the boys (especially Sam) were inclined to regard all promises unsubstantiated by hard proof as nothing but Airport.

However, Nick had decided that life as a one and only was not for him and he did not give up.

"Airport," said Sam when he described how one weekend the attic had been visited and his old cot rooted out. "Keep up the pressure!"

"You were right," Nick told him a week later. "They've forgotten that cot already. It's stuck in my bedroom blocking off the window. They're painting the spare room yellow now. It would make a jolly good baby's room."

"You should have told them so."

"I did."

"What did they say?"

"They said, 'Yes it would'. But it's probably only all Airport again. Mum has washed my old Peter Rabbit curtains and hung them in the window."

"Do not let them shut you up so easily," advised Sam, gazing meaningfully at the thinness of Nick's mother.

"They've even hung up a mobile," said Nick

"and they leave catalogues with prams in lying about for me to find."

"They must think you're daft!" said Sam. "But don't give up! It will be worth it in the end!"

Chapter Three

"Nick," said his mother. "About this baby."

"What baby?"

"The baby we talked about ages ago. You can't have forgotten! You must have seen us getting ready!"

"Peter Rabbit curtains and my old cot?"

"Yes," said his mother. "We shall be needing them again perhaps. I hope. After Christmas."

"After *Christmas?*" repeated Nick, very disappointed. For a moment his hopes had been raised. "But Christmas is ages away," he said.

"I suppose it is," agreed his mother. "And I didn't mean exactly straight after Christmas."

"After New Year?"

"Oh yes, after that."

"After we go back to school after New Year?"

"Oh yes. Probably after half-term, actually."

"After Christmas after New Year after we go back to school next year. After we go back to school next year's *half-term*?"

"Yes," said his mother.

"Airport," said Sam. "Poor old Nick!"

"Yes," agreed Nick. "I suppose they think I'll

have forgotten by then. Anything to shut me up! My mum even dragged me into Boots to look at baby clothes on Saturday!"

"Well, keep it up," said Sam. "It's either that or being a one and only and being run about after for the next ten years! Right through Big School! Poor old Nick!"

Christmas came closer and closer.

"Are they still doing it?" asked Sam. "Pretending about that baby to shut you up?"

"They haven't mentioned it lately," admitted Nick. "It's all Christmas talk now."

"Better ask again," said Sam.

"Are we still having that baby after Christmas?"

asked Nick, looking sternly at his mother, who despite three winter jumpers was still noticeably thinner than Mrs Oliver.

"Of course," said his mother laughing. "Didn't we tell you ages ago? Why do you think the spare room is being turned into a nursery? You're being a bit difficult, Nick!"

"Me?" said Nick, astonished.

"Did you eat your lunch?"

"All but the yogurt," said Nick.

Chapter Four

Nick's mother went to see Mrs Oliver.

"He won't believe it," she told her. "What else can we do? We've told him! We've created a nursery in front of his eyes! He can't seem to accept it."

"Perhaps," said Sam's mother, "you should drop the subject for a while."

"They've definitely given up on that baby idea,"

reported Nick gloomily. "It's completely off. It was all Airport; just like we thought. It's nothing but where we'll go for the summer holidays now."

"Never mind," said Sam comfortingly. "You're coming to stay with us at half-term. And your mum *is* getting fatter!"

"She's still a lot thinner than yours," said Nick, refusing to be cheered. "And do you know what they bought at the supermarket last night? Nappies! They must think I'm crackers!"

"Nick," said his father as he drove Nick and his luggage to Sam's house on the first morning of half-term. "You do realise, don't you?"

"Realise what?"

Nick's father sighed but said patiently, "This

baby. It could arrive any time now, you know."

"It's all right," said Nick kindly. "You don't have to keep it up, Dad. I've given up the baby idea."

"Too late now, old son," Mr Brown replied cheerfully.

"But I've been wondering. Couldn't we get a dog?"

"What?"

"I said, what about a dog?"

"Good grief!"

"It was just an idea," said Nick.

"Your dad," said Sam that afternoon, "is certainly stubborn! And your mum! Oh well, you will just have to make up your mind to be a one and only and run about after for the next ten years! That'll be right through Big School! Poor old Nick!"

"I'll give you Poor Old Nick!" exclaimed Mrs Oliver. "As soon as I get the twins and the baby to bed and have five minutes' peace I'm going to have a word with Poor Old Nick!"

However, before Mrs Oliver was anywhere near getting five minutes' peace, Nick's father was back, banging on the front door.

Sam answered it.

"A boy! A boy!" shouted Nick's father. "Another boy! Where's Nick? I want him now! Straight away! At once!"

"But we've just laid all my track out upstairs," protested Sam. "You said he could stay! He's only just come!"

"Go and fetch Nick at once!" said Mrs Oliver. "Really, Sam!"

"Your dad's here and he looks awful!" Sam told Nick. "What a mess! And he wants you straight away now at once. Might have known they'd never really let their one and only stop for half-term."

Nick's father drove the sulking Nick right across town. Right to the hospital. Marched him down miles and miles of corridors, shoved him through a swing door, led him to a bed. His mother was in it, holding a baby.

"Whose is it?" asked Nick, thinking, "Will they stop at nothing?"

"Ours!" shouted his father. "Ours! Yours! Your brother! Your new brother, Michael! Look, he's even got a label on! Michael Brown!"

"What an awful shock!" said Sam.

"Yes," agreed Nick. "They gave him to me

to hold and they said, 'Say something, Nick!' They were all laughing – Mum, Dad, the people in the other beds, nurses. They even brought in extra nurses to laugh! And they kept saying, 'Say something, Nick! Say something, Nick!'"

"They kept it very secret," said Sam. "They must have known for weeks! Months! So what *did* you say?"

"I said, 'Why didn't you tell me? Why didn't you *tell* me? WHY DIDN'T YOU TELL ME?'"

"Poor old Nick," said Sam.

PEDRO

Susan Price

Chapter One

Some boys and girls were running a race up the street. They fought through the gate of number forty-two, past the overgrown privet and elbowed each other aside as they ran up the path. They crowded into the little backyard all together, hot and out of breath, their hair everywhere and their socks falling down. Boys and girls, all together, knocked on the door.

It was answered by a thin, grey woman, wrapped up in a flowery pinafore dress.

All the children shouted together, "Please, Mrs Price, can Pedro come out to play?"

That Mrs Price was my great-gran, so I know this story is true.

Great-gran yelled, "Pedro!"

Pedro came running, rattley-tattley on the hard lino, throwing himself over the doorstep, racing round the yard, in and out of all the children, barking at the top of his voice and wagging his tail until he could hardly stand.

Pedro was a corgi.

The children would rush off down the path to the street, and Pedro would race ahead of them on his short little legs, barking like mad, and then run back to round them up.

"Come and skip with us, Pedro!"

"Come and play footer with us!"

There were hardly any cars about in those days, so it was safe to play in the road. The boys didn't have a proper football, so they played with a worn-out old tennis ball. Pedro would race after it,

dribbling it with his front paws. Or he'd leap into the air and head it.

One team would be kicking the ball towards the other team's goal when Pedro would snatch the ball up in his mouth and race down the street the other way.

"Oi, Pedro! You're on our side!"

Pedro could never remember what side he was on. Anyway, he usually dropped the ball before he got to the goal. One of the boys would kick it and away Pedro would go after it, barking, his little legs a blur.

It was a different kind of football – one with three teams. Our side, your side, and Pedro.

Then Pedro would see the girls skipping with a length of old clothes line, and he'd forget all about footer. He'd bounce up and down on the same spot on the pavement, going over the rope every time it came down. Every now and again he'd bark. The girls would try to keep up with him, but he was better than they were.

But Pedro didn't play fair. He would never take his turn at holding the rope. When Pedro got tired, he'd run back home. But – even if he'd been skipping – he'd always steal the ball from the footer game and take it with him. The boys would try to catch him, but he was a fast, nippy little dog, and could twist and turn and dive between their legs. He'd tear up the path to his house, the ball in his mouth and his ears turning inside out with his speed.

He'd knock on the kitchen door with his paw, and Great-gran would let him in. He'd shoot under the sideboard with the ball.

Then the children would be knocking at the door. "Please, Mrs Price, will you make Pedro give us our ball back?"

That was easier said than done.

Chapter Two

One of my great-gran's daughters, named Aileen, was courting a young man named Roman, who'd been a soldier in the War. He was Polish.

Roman came to Sunday tea. Great-gran got out her best cups and saucers, with roses painted on them.

Everyone sat round the table, and Great-gran poured out the first cup of tea. She put milk in it, and stirred in two lumps of sugar. Roman thought it would be for him, because he was the guest.

Great-gran passed the cup across the table to

him, but when he reached for it, she said, "That's for Pedro."

Roman sat there, holding the cup and saucer by the saucer's edge. He whispered to Aileen, "Who is Pedro?"

Aileen whispered back, "The dog."

Roman looked at the pretty cup and saucer, filled up with the milky, sugared tea. He often made mistakes with English, and thought he had made another one. "What?"

"The dog," Aileen whispered. "*Woof-woof!*"

In Poland, Roman had been told that the English were madder than bats and treated animals like people. And here he was, in a house full of mad English, having a mad tea-party. He thought he had better do what they said. So he stooped down, to put the cup and saucer on the lino for the dog.

"No, no!" Aileen whispered at him. "On the table!"

"But . . . " Roman had thought Aileen was a nice girl, but she was as mad as the rest. "You say is for the dog."

"On the table!" Aileen whispered. "Next to you."

So Roman put the cup and saucer at the place next to him at the table. There was an empty chair there, with two or three cushions on it.

Then the family dog jumped up onto the chair beside him. It sat on top of the cushions, put its paws on the edge of the table, poked its long snout into the little flowered cup, and began to drink its milky, sugared tea.

Then Great-gran took a tea towel off a big plate of boiled ham sandwiches. She put two on a dinner plate and passed it to Roman.

"That's for Pedro."

Roman couldn't believe that a dog was going to be given ham sandwiches on a plate. He sat holding the plate until Pedro – who was waiting with his paws on the edge of the table – barked at him.

Aileen whispered, "*Give* him his dinner."

Roman put the plate down on the floor, on the lino.

My great-gran stood up straight and put her hands on her hips. Aileen's brothers looked up from their comics. Her dad stopped drinking his tea.

Pedro, still at table, barked.

"A dog is not a man!" Roman said. "A dog should eat on the floor!"

Great-gran had the long carving knife in her hand, and she whacked the flat of it on the edge of the table.

"My lad," she said, "you shall eat your dinner on the floor if you've a mind, but in this family, we eat ours at the table."

Aileen snatched Pedro's plate up from the floor and put it on the table in front of him. She whispered to Roman, "Stop showing me up!"

Pedro gave Roman a long look, barked, and scoffed his sandwiches.

Roman went back to his lodgings, and told his Polish friends that it was all true – the English really were madder than bats.

Chapter Three

My great-gran's children hated Friday nights, because it was medicine night.

There was cod-liver oil. This came in a big, greasy bottle. The oil itself was greyish-green and smelled of fish, because it was made of cod's livers. Every Friday night everyone in the family – even my great-grandad – had to have a big tablespoonful of cod-liver oil. If one of her grown-up married children was visiting, they had to have a spoonful too – so they tried not to come on Friday nights.

The oil tasted of nothing much in a cold, nasty sort of way, and it was thick and slimy in the mouth.

Everyone had to line up, and Great-gran went along the line with her big spoon.

Pedro lined up with the rest, and he opened his mouth, and had the oil spooned down his throat, and was much better behaved about it than anyone else. He took his medicine like a corgi. Everyone else hated him on Friday nights, because while they were all pulling faces and retching and moaning, Pedro was so smug about it. He'd open up his black-ribbed throat, snap his white teeth, and the whole spoonful was down.

But worse was the Fenning's Fever Cure. My

great-gran was always worried about people catching fevers. If you hung about near drains, she said, you'd catch a fever. If you were out on a foggy night, you might catch a lung-fever. If you had a headache, she worried in case it turned into a brain-fever. So every Friday night everyone within her reach had to have a big tablespoonful of Fenning's Fever Cure, to cure them of whatever fever they might be about to catch.

I've never tasted this stuff myself – thank goodness – but I'm told that it was so bitter, so *nasty* that it made your tongue and every tooth in your mouth go rough and dry, and it made you shake from head to foot.

Everyone used to try to get out of the house before the Fenning's Fever Cure. My great-grandad tried to get off to the pub. Others used to think of errands to run, or people they had to see – but if you managed to escape, Great-gran would make you have *two* spoonfuls later on.

The only member of the family who never had to swallow a dose of Fenning's Fever Cure was Pedro.

"It's not fair," said my great-gran's sons and daughters. "He's so *good* about taking his cod-liver oil – let's see how he takes his Fenning's."

"You leave him alone," said Great-gran.

"He's so close to the ground," said Bill. "He'll breathe up a fever from a drain. Better give him some Fenning's."

"He's always a perfect little angel," Great-gran said.

It was so vexing, when you were shuddering and

screwing up your face after a spoonful of Fenning's, to open your eyes and see Pedro sitting on top of the cushions on his chair at the table, waiting for his last cup of tea before going to bed.

Roman told his friends at the Polish Club about Pedro going to bed. "Where does it sleep?" he said. "Does it sleep in the yard like a dog? No. Does it sleep on the floor in the house like a rich man's dog? No. It lies on the sofa, on its side, like a man, with its head on a pillow, and the old lady covers it over with a sheet and a blanket. It is true, it is true!" he said when everyone laughed. "And in the morning the old lady brings it a cup of tea in bed! I am not telling lies, nor stories! I have seen it!"

And Roman began to bring his Polish friends to tea. He told my great-gran it was because they wanted to taste her wonderful fruit cake, and she was very pleased, and used to give them a slice wrapped up in waxed-paper to take away with them. And her fruit cake was very good, and they enjoyed it – but the real reason they came was to see the mad English dog.

Chapter Four

The last part of the story is sad, I warn you. Pedro lived a long and very happy life, but he got old and sick. My great-gran wrapped him up in blankets, put him in an old pushchair and pushed him to the vet – which shows how much she loved him, because people hardly ever took their pets to the vet in those days. They were afraid that the bill would be too much for them to pay.

The vet said that Pedro hadn't long to live, and the kindest thing would be to put him to sleep. Great-gran couldn't bear that. So she pushed Pedro all the way home again. He went on getting sicker, though, and in the end she decided that the vet had been right. Still, she just couldn't face taking him back to the vet herself. She couldn't think about it without starting to cry.

So she went out into the street and called together the children who were playing there. "If I give you half-a-crown," she said, "will you take our Pedro to the vet and have him put to sleep?"

Half-a-crown was worth quite a bit – you could buy a lot of sweets with it in those days. The children agreed straight away. When my great-gran started to cry and said she couldn't take him, the boys all strutted and said *they* didn't care.

"I don't cry for nothing, I don't," one said.

"I wouldn't cry if it was me going to be put down," another one said.

So Great-gran wrapped Pedro up in blankets again, and put him in the pushchair. She handed him over to the children, and found half-a-crown for them from her purse. "You go slow with him and take good care of him," she said, and she stood crying in the street, watching them push him all the way along until they turned the corner.

Then she went back to her kitchen, sat at the table and cried and cried and cried, because she'd had Pedro for years, and now she'd never see him again.

When she'd cried all her tears out, it was hours later and quite dark. None of the children had come back to tell her what had happened – but perhaps they'd all gone home to their own houses.

Just then they came knocking at her back door. There they stood in a half-circle round her doorstep, all crying, and in the middle was the pushchair, with Pedro still in it.

All those tough boys, who wouldn't cry for

nothing, all rubbing their eyes with the backs of their hands or wiping them on their sleeves. "Have your half-crown back, Mrs Price."

"We couldn't."

"We don't want to do it, Mrs Price."

They hadn't got halfway to the vet. Then one had spoken up and said he didn't care if he didn't get any of the money, he wasn't going to do it. And one by one the others had agreed. But they'd promised Mrs Price, so they couldn't go back either. They'd walked round and round the streets for hours, pushing Pedro in the pushchair, until it got dark, and they had to go *somewhere*. So they'd come home instead.

"It's *Pedro*, Mrs Price."

★ ★ ★

I wish I could end this story by saying that Pedro got better, and went back to playing football and skipping, but I can't. He was a very old dog, and he was too sick to get better. What happened was that Great-gran put on her coat and pushed him round to the vet herself, and came home without him. And cried herself to sleep for a good many nights after.

That's the story almost as it was told to me, and almost every word of it is true.

THE MUCKITUPS

Robert Swindells

Chapter One

It was Saturday, and the Frimlys were busy as usual. Dad was on his knees, scrubbing the garden path. Mum had set up her handloom in the conservatory and was weaving. Eight-year-old Virginia was sketching a toadstool by the compost heap, and seven-year-old Dornford was plucking tiny weeds in his shrub garden. The sun was shining. The sky was blue. Everything was fine.

Presently Virginia thought she heard a motor. She cocked her head on one side. It *was* a motor, and it was getting closer. She stood up and leaned over the wall to see down Larkspur Drive, taking care not to dirty the cuffs of her top. A van came in sight. A very old van with purple and yellow paintwork and smoke belching out behind. It was the sort of van one didn't often see in Larkspur Drive, and Virginia was fascinated. She was even more fascinated when the vehicle rattled to a halt outside the empty house next door.

"Daddy!" she cried. "Come and see."

The van's nearside door creaked open and a big man stepped down in jeans and a chequered shirt.

There was a thick gold chain round his red neck and battered trainers on his feet.

As Virginia's father came down the path, wiping his hands on a towel, the man noticed her and winked. "Now then, sunshine."

Not knowing how to reply, Virginia smiled and nodded.

Her father nodded too. "Afternoon."

The big stranger grinned. "All right?"

Eric Frimly nodded again. "Fine, thanks. Can I help you at all?"

"Naw!" The man shook his shaggy head. "Moving in, that's all. Piece of cake. Have it done in a jiff."

"Oh . . . right." Her father's voice sounded strange and Virginia looked up at him as the two of them started back up the path.

"Is something the matter, Daddy?"

"What? Oh no, darling. Nothing's the matter." He didn't get the hose out though, to finish off the path as he usually did. Instead he went into the conservatory and said something to Mummy, and they both went indoors looking worried.

"Ginny?" Dornford had stopped weeding and was crossing Daddy's perfect lawn. "What's happening? Why has everybody stopped working?"

Virginia nodded towards the road. "New neighbours, Dorn."

"Oooh, goody!" Dornford's eyes sparkled. "I hope there's a boy like me. Oh – and a girl like you, of course. Let's go see."

Chapter Two

When they reached the wall, a woman was standing beside the man. She was nearly as big as he was. They were smoking and gazing at their new home. An empty cigarette packet lay on the pavement near their feet.

"Perfect," murmured the woman. "Isn't it perfect, Wayne?"

The man nodded. "Perfect, Hayley. Better start unloading."

As they crushed their cigarette ends under their feet and turned, they saw Dornford and Virginia.

Dornford said, "Have you got children, please?"

The woman nodded. "Yes, pet–four. Faron's nearly grown up now, but Darren, Karen and Sharon'll do for you. They're good kids. Muckitup's our name, by the way – Wayne and Hayley Muckitup."

"How d'you do," said Virginia. "We're called Frimly. He's Dornford, and I'm Virginia. Our parents are Eric and Freda. Daddy's in computers."

"Very nice," said Mrs Muckitup. "Wayne buys and

sells. Anything. *He's* in computers when any come his way." She smiled. "You'll have to excuse us now – lots of stuff to shift. We'll see you later, eh?"

"Oh, oh, yes of course," said Virginia. "Come on, Dorn."

They heard the van's shutter rattle up as they walked towards the house.

Next morning the Frimlys rose early, showered and put on their smartest outfits for church. As they walked to the Volvo, Dornford happened to glance into next door's garden. There, in a weed-choked strawberry bed stood a cracked lavatory bowl. He caught his father's sleeve. "Look, Daddy."

Daddy looked. So did Mummy.

"Good grief," said Daddy.

"Well exactly," said Mummy.

"Morning," said Wayne Muckitup, appearing round the side of the house lugging a stained mattress which he heaved into a stand of thistles. "Off out?"

"Church," said Eric, stiffly.

"Oh aye?" Wayne, fists on hips, contemplated the mattress. "Say one for me, will you?"

"You can come with us if you like," suggested Virginia. "The Volvo's very roomy."

Muckitup shook his head. "No ta, sunshine. I'm more of a feet-up-in-front-of-the-telly man, myself. Thanks all the same."

Inside the Volvo, Eric glared at his daughter. "In future, Virginia, I'd be obliged if you'd refrain from inviting that dreadful man to accompany us, to church or anywhere else. Is that clear?"

"But Daddy, he's our neighbour and the Bible says love thy neighbour."

Eric started the car. "The Bible does *not* say love them that do cast lavatory bowls upon the land, Virginia. What it *does* say, is honour thy father and thy mother, which means you do as I say. Understand?"

"Yes, Daddy."

Chapter Three

When they got back from church, the Frimlys changed into leisure wear and the children played quietly in the garden while Eric and Freda prepared breakfast. Presently the garden gate clicked and a little girl came clacking up the path in somebody's high heels.

"'Lo," she chirped. "I'm Sharon from next door."

"Virginia," said Virginia. "He's Dornford."

"Dornford?" Sharon looked at him. "What sort of a name's *that*?"

"It's *my* name," said Dornford, coolly.

"Well, you're welcome to it. Ciggy?" She held out a packet.

Virginia shook her head. "No, thanks – we don't. Cigarettes can damage your health."

Sharon nodded, taking one herself before stuffing the packet into her jeans pocket. "Very wise. Cutting down myself. First of the day, this." She produced a lighter, lit up and inhaled.

Dornford stared. "How old are you?"

"Eight. Why?"

"I wondered, that's all."

"Hmmm." Sharon looked around, smoke curling from her nostrils. "Nice garden."

Dornford nodded. "Not bad. Bit short on lavatory bowls, though. And mattresses." He pointed to a distant corner. "We're thinking of putting in a few old pushchairs over there to screen off that ugly bit of rockery."

"I could let you have one," offered Sharon. "We've got four."

Dornford started to explain that he'd been joking but before he could get the words out, Sharon had gone. She was back in less than a minute with a battered pushchair. The young Frimlys looked at each other, then at Sharon.

"Look – er – Sharon," said Virginia. "My brother was being sarcastic. You don't think *normal* people leave old pushchairs lying around their gardens, do you?"

Sharon sucked on her cigarette, blew out a plume

and watched it curl into the still air. "I don't know any normal people," she said. "But I thought *you* might go for it. You know – anything to brighten up your boring little lives."

"How *dare* you!" flared Virginia. "Our lives aren't the least bit boring."

Dornford looked at her. "Are you *sure* about that, Ginny? Sketching fungi? Watching Mummy weave? Singing Hebridean folksongs while other kids are watching telly? All that organic muesli? I think we ought to have the pushchair *and* an old lavatory bowl, if we can

find one. Come on, Ginny – don't be a spoilsport."

Virginia sighed. "I don't know, Dornford. It's not the pushchair so much as what it can *lead* to. Leave an old pram about and before you know it you're mixing with children called Dean and Craig and Kylie, watching *EastEnders* and eating at McDonald's. It's the thin end of the wedge, you see."

"Thin end of my granny!" growled Sharon, flicking her cigarette butt into the herbaceous border. "You want to loosen up, Ginny Frimly – start looking for fun." She swung a kick at a passing butterfly. "It's all round if you know where to look. I wouldn't sit drawing flipping toadstools all day if I was pretty like you."

Virginia looked at her. "Pretty? Me?"

Sharon nodded. "Sure. Touch of lipstick, some

proper clothes instead of that horrible stuff your mum's woven, you'd be pretty. Not like me – the ciggies have ruined *my* looks. Them and the Mars bar dinners.

"You have Mars bar *dinners*?"

"Oh aye – Mum doesn't like to cook, see? Gets the pans mucky, she says." Sharon grinned. "What about this pushchair, then?"

Virginia shrugged. Nobody had ever called her pretty before, and Mars bar dinners sounded scrummy, even if they *were* bad for you.

"All right, Sharon. We'll give it a try, but I shudder to think what Dad's going to say."

"If you think about it," said Dornford, "it's only the same as one of those wheelbarrows some people have. You know – painted white and filled with trailing plants. Only difference is, we've got four wheels instead of one."

They positioned the vehicle near the rockery and walked round it, studying it from various angles.

"Looks okay to me," said Sharon.

Virginia pulled a face. "Doesn't blend in somehow."

"Needs greenery," said Dornford. "Like those barrows."

They fetched pot plants from the greenhouse for
the pushchair's seat
and hung a basket
on its handle.
Virginia took a
cutting of mile-a-
minute and planted
it near a wheel where
it could take hold
and climb.
When Daddy
saw what was
happening he came
running out and
said no, but Mummy
was close behind him.

"Eric," she said, "the children *must* be permitted to express themselves." She didn't like the pushchair really, but Dornford and Virginia seemed to have found a friend in Sharon and they'd never had friends for long. Friends tended to laugh and eat sweets and run across the grass and Eric didn't encourage them. It was time they had a friend. If only she didn't smoke. Still, Virginia and Dornford might even persuade her to abandon the habit.

Next day after school, the young Frimlys got changed and hurried round to Sharon's to help her beautify the old lavatory. They filled the bowl with compost and Virginia said, "What plants have you got, Sharon?"

Sharon looked unhappy. "We don't have any plants," she said. "Only weeds." So they raided the Frimly rockery for stonecrop, thyme and aubrietia, which they planted in the compost. They stood back and looked.

"I love the way the aubrietia overhangs the rim,"

said Dornford, "but we need something round that pedestal. Something tallish."

They planted montbretia so that the pedestal was surrounded by slender, sword-like leaves.

When Sharon's dad came home, he stopped and stared. "By heck!" he growled. "You've made that lavatory even nicer than it was already." He pointed to where the front end of a car lay rusting in long grass. "P'raps you could do summat with *that*."

"Or this," said Faron, dragging an old gas cooker from the van.

"Oooh!" cried Virginia, "bags that for *our* garden. I could express myself *beautifully* on that."

So Faron hauled it next door and Virginia made a feature of it while Sharon and Dornford worked on the car. They were putting a nest-box under the

bonnet when eleven-year-old Darren appeared.

"What's that?"

"Nest-box," said Sharon

"What's it for?"

"To attract birds, of course," Virginia told him.

Darren grinned. "You mean bluetits and that?"

"Yes."

"Great! I *love* shooting bluetits, but they're too small and quick. They'll be sitting ducks in your nest-box."

"That's *not* the idea at all," sniffed Virginia. "We put in these boxes so we can *watch* the birds, not murder them."

"You watch bluetits?" Darren shook his head. "Don't know how you stand the excitement." He wandered off.

Chapter Four

Over the next few weeks the children divided all their free time between the two gardens. The Frimlys provided the plants and the Muckitups found the junk. There were TVs, freezers, juke-boxes, prams and armchairs, all to be positioned and decked with growing plants. Wayne even found an ancient mangle, and Virginia persuaded a convolvulus vine to twine its tendrils round and round the cracked wooden rollers.

The day came when Eric Frimly thought things had gone far enough but his wife wasn't sure, and anyway it was too late. "We can't go *back*, Eric," said Freda. "Progress, that's the thing."

So Eric stopped scrubbing the path and mowing the lawn and found he had more time for reading. Freda threw out her loom and spinning wheel and took up Tai Chi. Both became less tense. More fun. They still went to church but without dressing up for it, and sometimes Sharon came too. They decided their new neighbours weren't so bad after all – especially since they'd stopped smoking and

Darren now went armed with binoculars instead of his airgun. The loom and wheel became smothered in creeper, lawns vanished under the children's junk sculptures, moss grew on the path and nobody was uptight enough to care.

"You know, Hayley," said Wayne to his wife one Saturday afternoon, "I do believe moving in next to the Frimlys was the best move we ever made."

"Do you, pet?" murmured Hayley, nibbling a carrot stick.

"Definitely. Well, look at the garden for a kick-off. I never *knew* junk could look so good. See that lavatory bowl – like a Grecian urn, that is. And that fridge they sunk and filled with water. *Teeming* with fish and frogs. Our Karen's given up frog-trampling since we've had that. There's even a water-lily in it. Surrounded by nature, that's what we are. And they were right about the ciggies, and all. We're a hundred quid a week better off since we kicked that filthy habit. Our *Sharon* was getting through thirty a day. Now look at her – no coughing in the mornings, spitting all over the floor. You can walk in your bare feet now without treading in—"

"Wayne!" Hayley wagged a finger. "*Some* things we don't talk about in Larkspur Drive."

"Sorry, love," smiled Wayne, "but there you are –

there was *nothing* we didn't talk about, and at the top of our voices too, till we came here."

Virginia and Dornford? Well, they'd never been popular kids, with their fussy parents and prissy ways. Not to mention their weird names. The Muckitups christened them Gin and Dor and they never looked back. If they got their hands dirty, they got their hands dirty. If they tore their clothes, so what? They had friends they could invite in without Mum fussing. Nobody *cared* about footprints on the parquet, crumbs down the three piece suite. Kids are kids. Let 'em make a mess and be happy. And if they want a rumpus in the garden, why not – it's full of junk already.

★ ★ ★

The best thing happened in August, when the annual Glorious Gardens competition took place. The Frimlys had won before, of course – a really boring win in the Cleanest Path category. In fact, they'd won it every year till now. This time, when the judges saw the moss and the tufts of grass sprouting in the cracks, they looked at one another, wrinkled up their noses and shook their heads. But when they saw what the children had created from junk, they awarded the Frimlys and the Muckitups joint first place in the Novelty section.

That night the two families threw a party. A garden party.

They ate, drank and sang. They danced and popped party poppers and wore silly hats and chased one another round and round the fridges and the cookers and the pushchairs. They didn't smoke or swear or get drunk but they had a wonderful time, which just goes to show something or other.

At midnight, Wayne raised his glass of carrot juice and yelled, "Hey, how about a toast – to the Frimlys!"

Everybody drank, then Eric Frimly climbed on top of a car which was held together by its covering of sweet peas. His hair was messy and his shirt tail was out. He lifted the old jam jar he was drinking from and bellowed, "The Muckitups!" before missing his mouth and pouring dandelion and burdock down the front of his shirt.

"THE MUCKITUPS!" roared everybody, so loudly that the bats who lived in the Frimlys' spare bedroom went skittering into the night.

JIMMY JELLY

Jacqueline Wilson

Chapter One

Do you ever watch Jimmy Jelly on the telly? My little sister Angela is crazy about him.

She doesn't usually watch children's programmes.

She only watches Jimmy Jelly. She laughs at all his jokes though she doesn't understand them. I'm eight, but I don't always understand them myself actually.

She tries to join in when he sings his silly songs.

She jumps up and down when he does his daft

wobble jelly dance.

She records every single one of his shows and then she watches him over

and over

and over again until it's time for his next show.

It drives Mum and me mad.

I can't stand Jimmy Jelly. And neither can Mum. We like to watch real-life television programmes.

"Boring," says Angela.

She runs round the room and makes a racket whenever there's anything *we* want to watch.

I get annoyed.

Mum gets annoyed.

Mum gets very cross with Angela.

I can't stand it when Mum gets cross with me. I get very red in the face. Sometimes (this is a secret) I even cry.

Angela gets red in the face but she never cries when Mum tells her off. Sometimes she laughs, though this makes Mum get *really mad*. Angela still doesn't care. My little sister Angela is only four but she can be very *fierce*.

Mum generally wins the battle, but only just. Angela stops running round the room. She sits on the sofa with us. But she doesn't half fidget.

She stops shouting. But she doesn't keep totally quiet. She *mutters*.

We can't make out exactly what she's saying. Just the odd word or two.

"Mumble mumble mumble Jimmy Jelly," Angela

mutters. "Jimmy Jelly mumble mumble mumble."

"Stop mumbling, Angela," says Mum.

Angela glares at her. She stays quiet for a few seconds. Then, "Hiss hiss hiss Jimmy Jelly," Angela hisses. "Jimmy Jelly hiss hiss hiss."

"Angela!" says Mum, turning the telly up louder.

"I thought I told you to stop mumbling?"

"I'm not mumbling. I'm whispering," says Angela.

"It's the first sign of madness, mumbling to yourself," I say.

"I'm not mumbling to myself. I'm talking to Jimmy Jelly," says Angela.

"What do you mean, you're talking to Jimmy

Jelly?" I say. "He's not on the telly now. It's another programme."

"Yes, and we're missing it," says Mum. "Shh!"

"I *know* he's not on the telly," says Angela. "He's squeezed out of that boxy bit at the back of the telly and he's come to visit me."

"Oh yes?" I say. "So where is he then? I can't see him."

"Of course *you* can't see him," says Angela. "I'm the only one who can see him because he's *my* Jimmy Jelly. And budge up a bit on the sofa, Rosie, because you're squashing him."

"You're crazy," I say.

"She's the one that's crazy, isn't she, Jimmy Jelly?" says Angela.

"You're all driving *me* crazy," says Mum, turning

the telly up again. "I've had a hard day at work and now I just want to relax."

"Yes, I've had a hard day at school and *I* just want to relax," I say.

"Yes, I've had a hard day at play and Jimmy Jelly and I want to relax," says Angela.

Angela plays round at our nan's house on Mondays. She goes to Aunty Pat's on Tuesdays. She goes to Aunty Jean's on Wednesdays. She goes to Mrs Brown up the road on Thursdays. She goes to playschool on Fridays.

They all say they think the world of our Angela but they can only cope with her one day a week. Now they have to cope with Angela *and* Jimmy Jelly.

Angela and Jimmy Jelly sing silly songs when our nan needs a nap.

Angela and Jimmy Jelly jump up and down in Aunty Pat's small flat.

Angela and Jimmy Jelly tell joke after joke when Aunty Jean has a headache.

Angela and Jimmy Jelly say they don't like Mrs Brown's nice rice pudding and insist they only eat jelly.

Angela and Jimmy Jelly get all the other children at playschool to tell their jokes and sing their songs and jump up and down doing their daft wobble jelly dance.

And Mum and me have to put up with Angela and Jimmy Jelly at teatime

and bathtime

and bedtime

and all day Saturday!

Chapter Two

Guess what happens on Sundays? Angela leaves Jimmy Jelly at home. We see our dad on Sundays.

Ages ago we were one big family, Mum and Dad and me and Angela. She was just a little baby then. Though she was still fierce.

But then Mum and Dad split up because they had a lot of rows. Angela and I have a lot of rows too, but children don't get divorced. So now we're two small families. We're Mum and me and Angela on Mondays, Tuesdays, Wednesdays, Thursdays, Fridays and Saturdays.

Dad comes and collects us for the day on Sundays. And then we're Dad and me and Angela.

Mum stays at home. And so does Jimmy Jelly.

Angela kisses Jimmy Jelly goodbye. She kisses him very fondly, lots and lots of times.

Dad didn't know what she was doing at first. He doesn't always understand. He especially doesn't understand Angela.

"Angela? What on earth are you doing? Why are you making those weird kissing noises?"

"I'm saying goodbye to Jimmy Jelly," says Angela.

"Jimmy who?" says Dad. He doesn't watch television very much.

"Jimmy Jelly on the telly," I say.

"I've never heard of him," says Dad.

"Then you're very lucky," says Mum. "We've certainly heard of him, haven't we, Rosie?"

"I'll say," I say, sighing.

"You go back inside the telly, Jimmy Jelly," says Angela. "You stay there till I get home."

She gives him one last kiss when he's back inside the telly.

"Angela! You're making the screen all smeary," says Mum.

"Bye bye, Jimmy Jelly," says Angela, waving at the blank screen. "Don't be lonely. You can pop out and see Mum for a bit if you really want."

"Ooh, goodie goodie!" says Mum.

"But you're not to get *too* friendly. You're *my*

Jimmy Jelly," says Angela.

"Are you quite done?" says Dad wearily. "Can we go now?"

"Yes, Dad," says Angela, and she takes hold of his hand. "I'll give you a hello kiss now I've given all my goodbye kisses to Jimmy Jelly."

We always have a good day out with Dad on Sundays.

Sometimes we go to the park.

Sometimes we go to the river.

Sometimes we go all the way to the seaside.

We always eat a lot of lunch.

We have a lot of snacks too.

Angela sometimes feels sick when it's time to go home.

Angela sometimes *is* sick.

She was sick all over me.

"It's a good job Jimmy Jelly stayed at home," she said. "He'd have got sicked on too. And he doesn't like sick."

"I don't like sick either!" I said, mopping me and mopping Angela.

Dad isn't very good when it comes to mopping. But he does give us good days out.

Mum has a good day in.

Sometimes she goes back to bed for an extra snooze.

She reads the Sunday newspapers.

She listens to the radio.

She gardens.

She tries on all her clothes.

She watches the telly.

She doesn't watch Jimmy Jelly. He stays inside. Still and silent.

But he comes rushing out the minute Angela and I get back from our day out with Dad.

Chapter Three

"We're going to the shopping centre on Saturday," says Mum.

"Oh good," I say. I like shopping.

"Oh bad," Angela says. She hates shopping.

"No, Angela, you're going to want to come this special Saturday," says Mum, waving the local paper at us.

She shows us this big photo on the front.

"Who's this, Angela?" says Mum.

Angela stares. "It's Jimmy Jelly!" she says.

"That's right! Jimmy Jelly is coming to our shopping centre this Saturday. He's opening up this big new music shop," says Mum.

Angela looks very surprised. "He didn't say anything about it to me," she says.

"No, darling, this is the *real* Jimmy Jelly. You'll be able to see him on Saturday," says Mum.

"I can see him any day I want," says Angela. She puts her arm up and hugs thin air. "Can't I, Jimmy Jelly?"

Mum shakes her head and sighs to me. "Maybe she's too little to understand, Rosie," she says. "Never mind. Just wait till Saturday. She'll be so excited."

Angela doesn't *act* excited on Saturday. She makes a fuss when Mum tries to hurry her up.

"Switch the telly off, Angela, and run and get your clothes on," says Mum.

"But I want to watch Jimmy Jelly!"

"We're going to see the real Jimmy Jelly, Angela, I keep telling you. That's why we want to go to the shopping centre early. So we can get a good place at the front of the crowd," says Mum.

There are crowds and crowds and crowds down at the shopping centre. Mum holds our hands tightly in case we get lost. Angela wriggles and fusses and tries to pull her hand away.

"No, Mum. I'm holding Jimmy Jelly's hand," says Angela.

At the sound of Jimmy Jelly's name all the heads

turn and stare at my little sister. They think she's maybe *really* holding Jimmy Jelly's hand. Mum and I grin and giggle. Angela glares.

"I don't like all these people," she moans. "I'm getting squashed."

"Here, darling, you squeeze in front of me," says a kind lady.

There are lots of kind ladies. It's not long before Angela is right at the front. And Mum and me.

"Aren't we lucky, girls?" says Mum.

"Why?" says Angela. "This is boring just standing and I'm still getting squashed."

"Stop moaning, Angela," I say. "Jimmy Jelly's going to be here in a minute."

"There he is!" Mum says, pointing.

"Jimmy Jelly!" everyone shouts.

Jimmy Jelly jumps up onto the platform and waves and smiles at everyone.

"Wave, Angela," says Mum. "It's Jimmy Jelly!"

Mum waves. I wave. All the crowd waves. All the crowd except Angela.

"Hi, everyone," says Jimmy Jelly. "It feels strange stuck up here all on my ownsome. Who wants to come and keep me company, eh?"

He peers all round the crowd. Mum pushes Angela forward.

"Here's your number one fan, Jimmy Jelly," says Mum, and she lifts Angela onto the platform.

"Hi there, poppet. What's your name, eh?" says Jimmy Jelly.

Angela lowers her head and presses her lips together. She doesn't say a word.

"Angela! Tell Jimmy Jelly your name," I hiss.

Jimmy Jelly looks at me. And Mum.

"Come on, girls," he says, helping us up onto the platform too.

We tell Jimmy Jelly our names.

We laugh when Jimmy Jelly tells a joke.

We join in when he sings his silly song.

We jump up and down when he does his daft wobble jelly dance.

We know exactly what to do because we've watched him over and over again.

Angela knows what to do too. But she doesn't do it. She doesn't do anything. She just stands there. She won't laugh, she won't sing, she won't dance.

"I'm ever so sorry, Jimmy Jelly," says Mum. "I don't know what's up with her."

"Never mind, I expect she's just a bit shy," says Jimmy Jelly, and he picks Angela up and gives her a kiss.

Angela goes very pink, but she still doesn't say a word.

Jimmy Jelly gives me a kiss too.

And Mum.

And he gives us a signed Jimmy Jelly poster and Jimmy Jelly badge and a Jimmy Jelly balloon.

Everyone stares at us as we climb down from the platform. It's as if we're almost as famous as Jimmy Jelly.

"Oh goodness, weren't we lucky?" says Mum.

"He's much nicer than I thought, old Jimmy Jelly," I say.

But Angela still says nothing at all.

"Whatever's the matter with you, Angela?" says Mum. "You're not usually shy."

"I'm *not* shy," says Angela.

"So why on earth didn't you talk to Jimmy Jelly?" I say.

"That wasn't Jimmy Jelly!" says Angela.

"Of course it was, Angela," says Mum.

"That wasn't *my* Jimmy Jelly," says Angela. "I didn't like *that* Jimmy Jelly one bit."

She doesn't even want to wear the Jimmy Jelly badge or carry the Jimmy Jelly balloon.

So I have them instead.

I want the poster too, to pin over my bed.

"No, I want the poster," says Mum. "You've got the badge and balloon, Rosie."

We argue about it all the way home.

"Those two are driving me crazy," says Angela to her Jimmy Jelly.

Then we all squash up on the sofa and watch Jimmy Jelly on telly.